DISNEY PRINCESS

This Disney Princess
Annual belongs to

Emma

Write your name here.

DISNEP PRINCESS

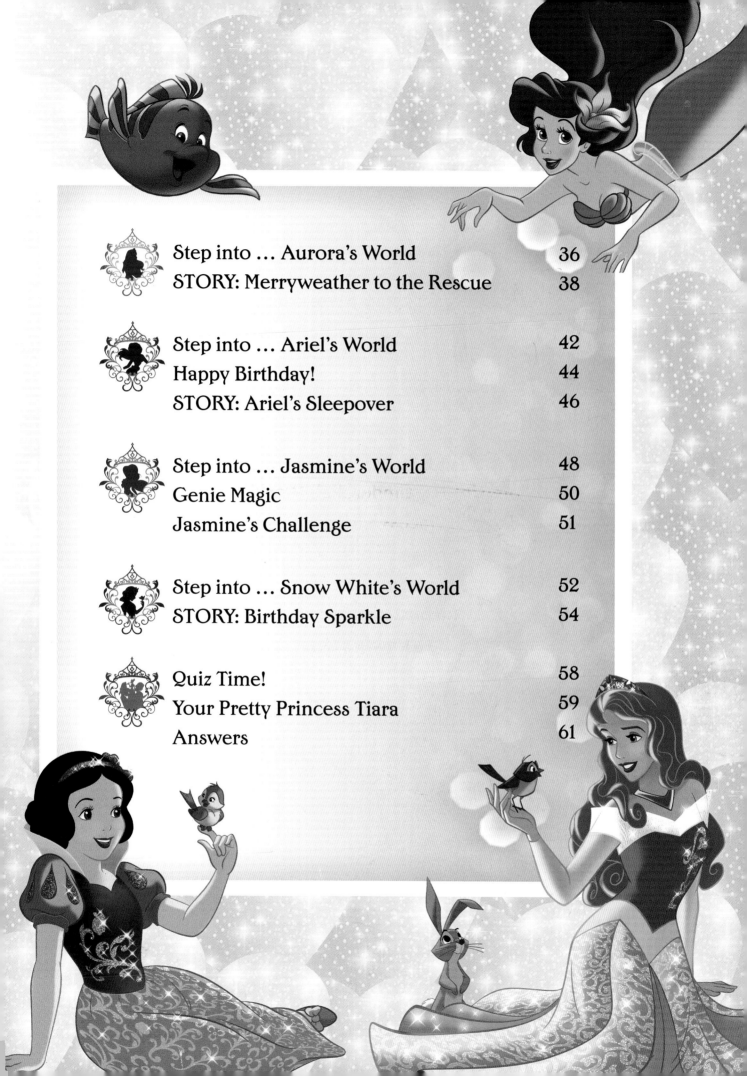

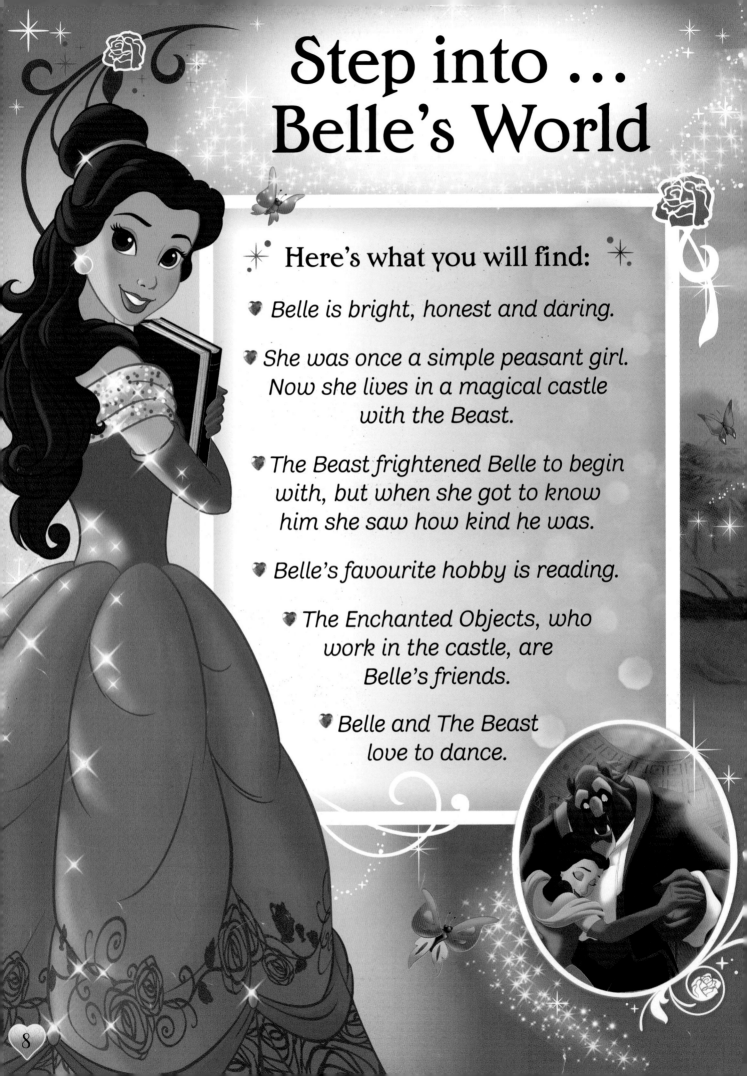

Step into ... Belle's World

Here's what you will find:

♥ Belle is bright, honest and daring.

♥ She was once a simple peasant girl. Now she lives in a magical castle with the Beast.

♥ The Beast frightened Belle to begin with, but when she got to know him she saw how kind he was.

♥ Belle's favourite hobby is reading.

♥ The Enchanted Objects, who work in the castle, are Belle's friends.

♥ Belle and The Beast love to dance.

Colour in this picture of Belle with her friends, Mrs Potts and Chip.

The Wardrobe makes all Belle's beautiful dresses. Can you spot her on this page?

Make friends with Belle

If Belle came to my house, we would play:

BELLE

....

Answer on page 61.

In the Palace Garden

Belle is enjoying her book so much that she doesn't notice what is going on in the garden. See what you can spot!

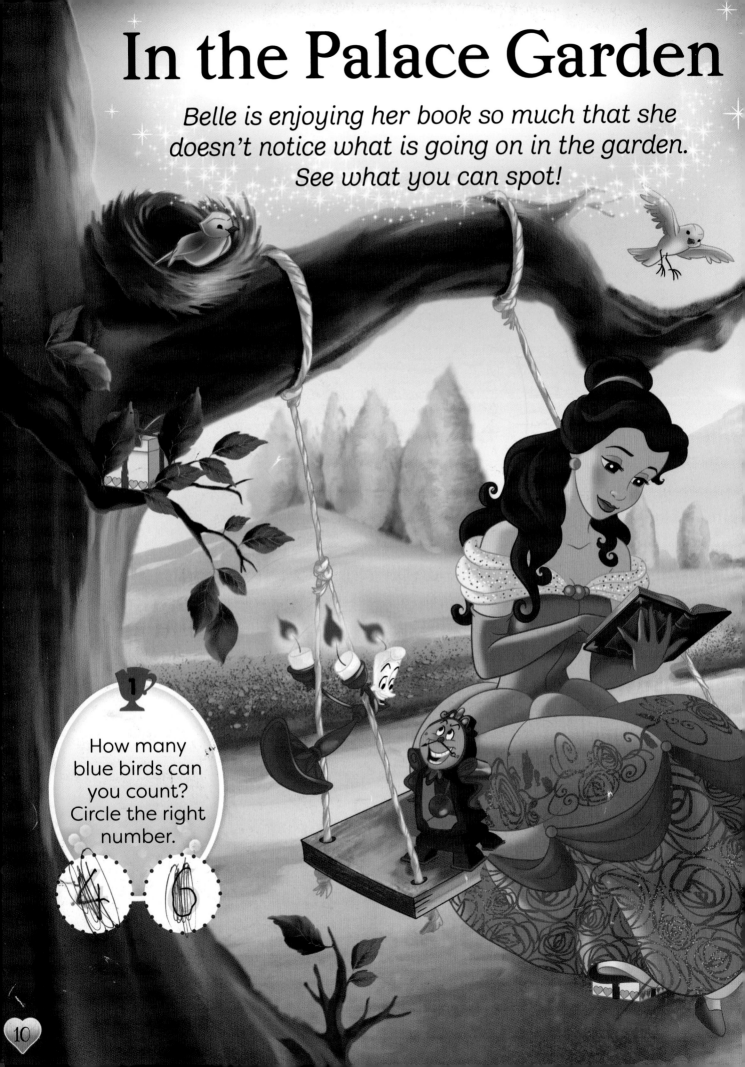

How many blue birds can you count? Circle the right number.

2 Point to the Beast who is having fun hiding.

3 Can you find these three presents?

4 Circle the object that isn't in the garden.

a   b

5 Cogsworth is on the swing. Tick the right answer.

True   False

Answers on page 61.

Building Bridges

1 One morning, Belle was shopping in the village square when she came across a poster for a contest. Belle thought a contest sounded like fun!

2 The poster said that the bridge across the river was too low for boats to pass under. The town elders would give a prize to whoever could design a new bridge to solve the problem.

Contest

Draw a prize trophy on this poster.

3 "Hello, Belle," said Gaston. "Guess who is going to win this contest?" "I don't know," said Belle, "but I read about a bridge that could open for boats and..."

12

4 "You and your silly books," laughed Gaston. "I will win this contest!" said Belle. She went to ask her father, the inventor, for help with her idea.

5 "How about making a drawbridge?" said Belle. "You pull the ropes and the bridge goes up." "It's a splendid idea," said her father. "Let's join the contest together!"

6 Belle and her father got straight to work building a model bridge to show the town elders their idea. They worked late into the night.

1 Where did Belle get the idea for the bridge?

a

b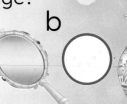

c

13

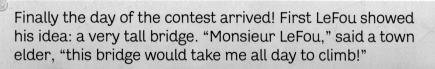

7 Finally the day of the contest arrived! First LeFou showed his idea: a very tall bridge. "Monsieur LeFou," said a town elder, "this bridge would take me all day to climb!"

8 Then Belle and Maurice showed their design. "Our drawbridge can be opened from the boat." The judges studied it, but Belle still wasn't sure if they would win...

9 Next, Gaston proposed to the town elders that they should tear down the old bridge and just let everyone swing on a rope across the river!

a   b   c

2

Who do you think should win the prize for best design?

10 Unfortunately, Gaston didn't quite make it to the other side of the river.

11 Finally the town elders announced their winner. "The prize goes to..." announced the town elder, "...Maurice and Belle!" The villagers cheered and Maurice beamed with pride. Belle felt so happy that she could use what she learned in books to help the people of her village!

The End

Can you draw your own bridge over the river?

Answers on page 61.

Fun on the Swing

These pictures look the same, but there are five differences in the bottom one. See if you can find them.

a

Colour in a rose when you spot a difference.

b

Answers on page 61.

Brave and Beautiful Belle

Gentle and Genuine Cinderella

Best Friends

Trace the letters to find out what Cinderella's animal friends think of her.

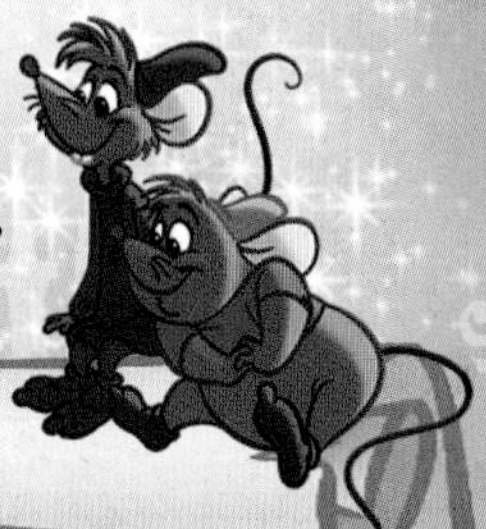

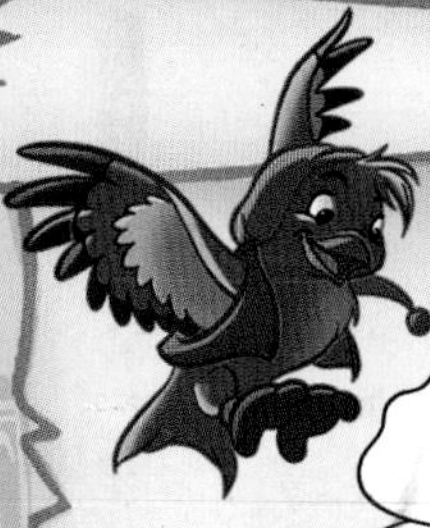

We love Cinderella because she is:

kind

caring

calm

Colour the flowers if you agree!

Answers on page 61.

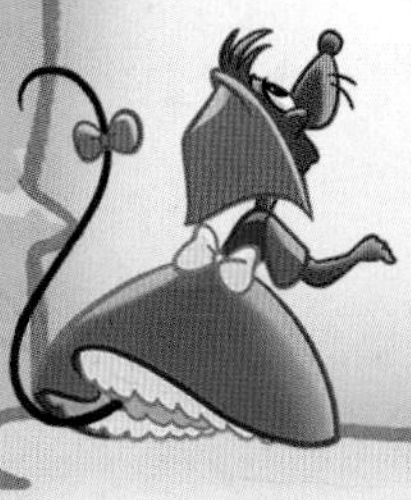

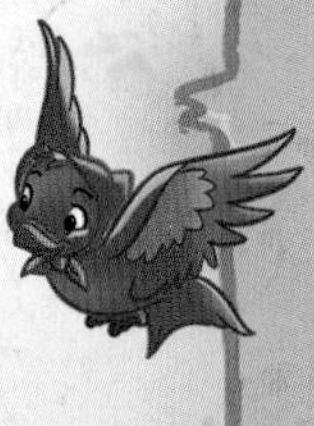

Step into ...
Cinderella's World

Here's what you will find:

♥ Cinderella is kind to her animal friends, hardworking and ever hopeful.

♥ Her two step-sisters were mean to Cinderella, but she kept on dreaming of a better life.

♥ The Fairy Godmother used her magic to send Cinderella to the ball.

♥ At the ball Cinderella danced with Prince Charming! But she had to leave before the magic wore off.

♥ 'Cinderelly' is what Gus and Jaq (the mice) call Cinderella. They are her special friends.

Join the dots on Cinderella's dress, then add some fairytale colours.

How many mice can you count on the page?

Share your wish with Cinderella

My special wish is:

Answer on page 61.

Playful Princess

Join Cinderella having fun with her friends and help her solve these puzzles.

Whose Shadow?

Draw a line to match each character with its shadow.

a

b

c

d

1

2

3

4

Slipper Count

How many glass slippers are there? Write the number below.

There are [ ] glass slippers.

Rosy Fun

Jaq wants to give Cinderella a rose. Can you find the two matching pictures?

a

b

c

d

e

f

Answers on page 61.

23

Teatime Treasure

*Can an old map lead Cinderella and
her friends to hidden treasure?*

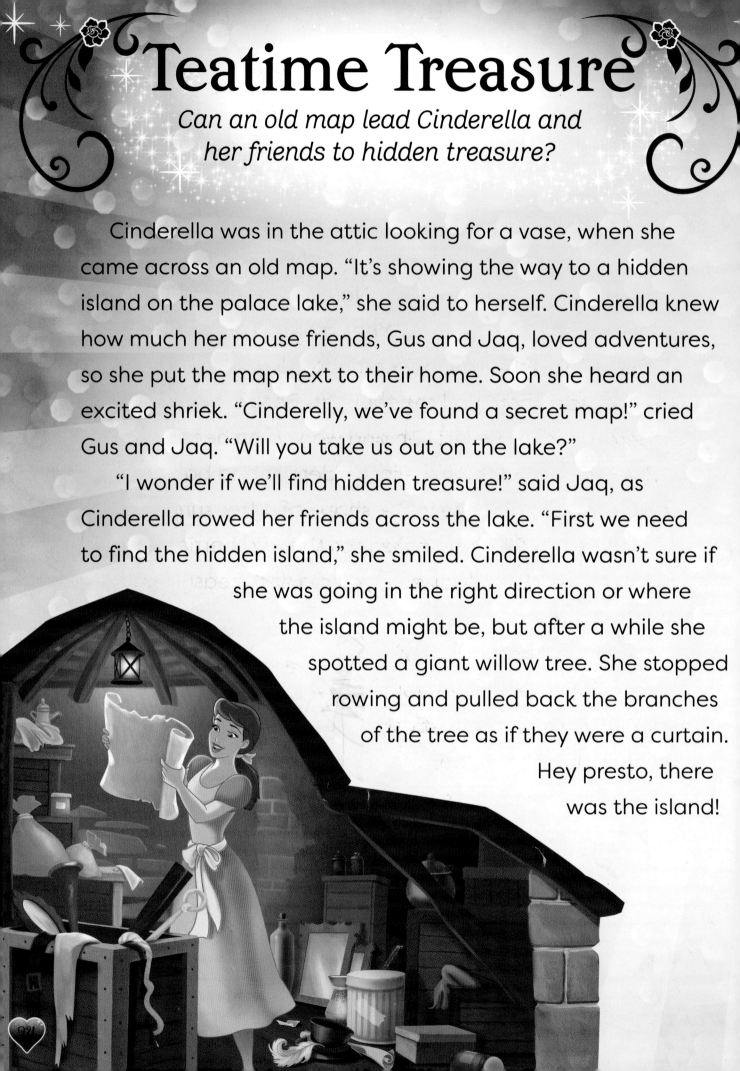

Cinderella was in the attic looking for a vase, when she
came across an old map. "It's showing the way to a hidden
island on the palace lake," she said to herself. Cinderella knew
how much her mouse friends, Gus and Jaq, loved adventures,
so she put the map next to their home. Soon she heard an
excited shriek. "Cinderelly, we've found a secret map!" cried
Gus and Jaq. "Will you take us out on the lake?"

"I wonder if we'll find hidden treasure!" said Jaq, as
Cinderella rowed her friends across the lake. "First we need
to find the hidden island," she smiled. Cinderella wasn't sure if
she was going in the right direction or where
the island might be, but after a while she
spotted a giant willow tree. She stopped
rowing and pulled back the branches
of the tree as if they were a curtain.
Hey presto, there
was the island!

Gus and Jaq were thrilled and instantly jumped out of the boat. The three friends searched the island for treasure, but all they found were pieces of old wood and lots of wild berries.

"Nothing," said Gus, sadly. "What a disappointment."

Cinderella felt sorry for her friends. "I must think of an idea to cheer them up," she thought. Back at the palace, Cinderella hid in the kitchen and worked on her surprise.

Then she called the mice in. Cinderella had baked a healthy, tasty fruit cake in the shape of a treasure chest. She had filled the cake with the wild berries they'd found on the island. "You see, you did find treasure after all!" she laughed.

They all had a slice of the special cake. "Thank you, Cinderella. This is the tastiest treasure ever!" said Jaq.

"Nature is full of treasures," Cinderella replied, "and they don't have to be gold or jewels to be wonderful!"

The End

Step into ... Rapunzel's World

Here's what you will find:

- *Playful and curious, Rapunzel is never afraid to try anything.*

- *She is creative and loves to paint.*

- *Rapunzel goes on an adventure with Flynn Rider, a charming thief.*

- *Pascal is Rapunzel's friend. He's a green chameleon who can change colour.*

- *Lanterns in the sky mark special moments in Rapunzel's story.*

- *Flynn helped Rapunzel realise she was the lost princess.*

Can you find Pascal? He's in disguise!

Make this picture even more fun by colouring it in!

What a pretty name!

Trace the letters.

Rapunzel

Answer on page 61.

27

Pascal's Portrait

Read this story using the pictures below to help you.

sun   Pascal   paintbrushes   Maximus

The  was out and Rapunzel decided to paint a portrait of her friend, . She set out her  then looked for . She wanted him to sit by the window so that her picture showed the  shining. "" she called. "Where are you?"  was hiding under the bed. Rapunzel realised that the cheeky chameleon was up to mischief.

"Oh dear," sighed Rapunzel loudly. "Now, I'll just have to use my  to paint , instead."

jumped up in surprise. Rapunzel musn't paint

's portrait instead of his! He leapt onto the

windowsill and gave Rapunzel a big, friendly smile.

"There you are," laughed Rapunzel. "Now sit still in the

bright and I shall get started." did as he was

told. He wanted Rapunzel to paint the best portrait ever!

The End

Help Rapunzel colour the painting of Pascal.

Flower Trail

Rapunzel has been drawing some of her favourite things. Now they need some colour.

Follow the trail. How many golden flowers are there?

8

Use your favourite colours here!

30

Answer on page 61.

Stand Still, Maximus!

Rapunzel and Flynn like the butterflies, but Maximus isn't so sure.

Match the jigsaw pieces to the spaces in the picture. Draw a line to where each one belongs.

a

b

c

d

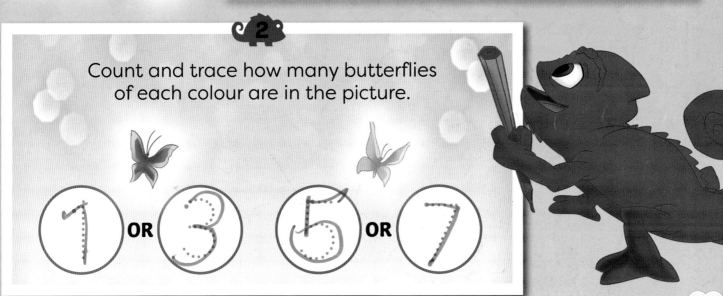

Count and trace how many butterflies of each colour are in the picture.

1 OR 3   5 OR 7

Answers on page 61.

Step into ... Tiana's World

Here's what you will find:

♥ *Tiana is talented, confident and really believes in herself.*

♥ *She worked hard to open her own restaurant, Tiana's Palace.*

♥ *Tiana met Prince Naveen when he had been turned into a frog!*

♥ *Kissing him, unexpectedly turned Tiana into a frog, too!*

♥ *Tiana and Charlotte have been best friends since they were little girls.*

♥ *Tiana loves cooking, as well as being a princess.*

Which of these pictures is Prince Naveen?

a

b

Get out your green colouring pencils for this picture of Tiana and her frog prince.

Tiana's palace

What's cooking?

Tick what you would like to make with Tiana:

Answer on page 61.

It's Snow Time

Tiana and Naveen are visiting a faraway country, where the snow is beautiful but very c-c-c-old!

a   b   c

f

e

d

1

Pretty Flakes

Can you pair up the matching snowflakes?

2

Sweet Angel

Trace over the lines to help Tiana finish her snow angel.

Try this
Draw a face on the angel.

Cosy Boots

Naveen has bought Tiana a pair of winter boots. Colour them in to match her coat.

Make a Snowman

Use this space to draw a jolly snowman.

Try this
Add these things to your picture.

Answers on page 61.

Step into ... Aurora's World

Here's what you will find:

- Aurora is cheerful, graceful and gentle.

- She loves to sing and dance with her forest creature friends.

- Aurora grew up thinking she was a peasant girl called Briar Rose.

- Flora, Merryweather and Fauna are Aurora's kind Fairy Godmothers.

- Aurora was 16 when Maleficent's spell sent her into a deep sleep.

- Prince Phillip's kiss broke the evil curse.

Circle the smallest and biggest rose.

a   b   c

d

Colour in Aurora dancing with her friends.

Swirl and Twirl!

Make up your own dance, swirling and twirling around the room, just like Aurora!

Answer on page 61.

37

Merryweather to the Rescue

1 One early morning Aurora heard a strange sound coming from the meadow. She followed the sound and discovered a little lamb stuck in some vines. "You poor dear!" said Aurora.

Baaaaa, baaaaa!

2 Aurora quickly untangled the vines from the lamb's legs. "Now we've got to find your mother," said Aurora. "Baaaaa, baaaaa," bleated the lamb. "I'm glad to hear that you agree," laughed Aurora.

3 Aurora took the lamb to the three fairies. They thought she was adorable and wanted to help look for her mother.

4

The fairies searched the countryside with Aurora. "Look!" cried Merryweather, pointing to a goat. "It's the lamb's mother." "That's not her mother, silly," said Flora. "That's a goat!"

5

As they passed by a meadow, a mother deer watched her young play. "Is that the lamb's mother?" asked Merryweather, hopefully. "Whoever heard of a lamb with a deer for a mother?" laughed Fauna.

6

But when the little lamb saw the deer, she joined in with their game. Aurora suggested that the fairies fly instead of walking to find the lamb's mother faster.

7

Aurora and the lamb would wait in the meadow. "That's a fine idea," said Flora. "As long as Merryweather promises not to bring back a mother bear for the little lamb!"

8

The fairies each flew off in a different direction. As Merryweather zipped along, she spotted a herd of sheep! She was sure one of them was the lamb's mother, but which one?

9

Merryweather rushed back to tell Aurora the good news. But when she arrived, the lamb was still busy playing with the young deer.

10

Merryweather could see that the lamb thought the deer was its mother. How would she ever get the lamb to leave and find her real mother?

Oh dear!

11

Instead of bringing the lamb to the sheep herd, Merryweather decided to bring the sheep herd to the lamb! So she buzzed about herding the sheep towards the meadow.

To everyone's astonishment, Merryweather managed to herd all of the sheep into the meadow! Suddenly, a sheep ran up to the little lamb. There was no doubt; this was the lamb's mother. "You've saved the day, Merryweather!" said Aurora, happily. "Baaaaa, baaaaa!" agreed the little lamb.

Come along this way!

The End

Draw a line to match each baby animal to its right mother.

a   b   c   d   e

1   2   3   4   5

Answers on page 61.

Step into ...
Ariel's World

Here's what you will find:

- Ariel is curious, lots of fun and free-spirited!

- She is a mermaid who longed to know about the human world.

- When Ariel rescued Prince Eric from the sea, she didn't realise she would end up being his princess!

- King Triton is Ariel's father. He didn't want her to leave her underwater home.

- Ariel's best friend is a cute little fish called Flounder.

- Ariel's lovely singing voice is very special to Prince Eric.

Match the shadow of the shell.

a   b

c

Add some splashy colour to this sweet picture!

This little mermaid is called:

Trace the letters.

Ariel

Answer on page 61.

Happy Birthday!

It's Flounder's birthday and Ariel has set him a treasure hunt.

Start

Join in the fun and wish Flounder Happy Birthday!

Stop off to colour in the oyster.

Trace over the dolphin's trail!

a

b

c

d

3

Spot which turtle is the odd one out.

1 Which is the smallest fish in this school of fish?

b

a

c

d

e

f

2 Follow the cheeky dolphin and count its jumps.

4 Ariel has hidden Flounder's present. Can you find it?

Finish

Answers on page 61.

Ariel's Sleepover

*An evening of fun and games turns
into a rescue mission for Ariel.*

King Triton was going away for the night. "My trident
will keep you safe, but do not let it fall into the wrong
hands," he told Ariel and her sisters.

The mermaids decided to have a sleepover. They did not
realise that Ursula, the sea witch, was planning some fun
of her own. Later that day, an old pedlar arrived at the palace
with pretty things to sell. Ariel bought a music box from her.

At the sleepover, Ariel opened
the music box to play and went
to make sea fruit smoothies.
When she returned, all her sisters
were asleep. Ariel noticed some
strange music playing from her
music box. "The music is making
everyone go to sleep," she
realised. Ariel quickly closed
the lid of the box. Then she
saw that her father's trident
was missing! "Oh no!" she cried.

Suddenly, she spotted Ursula's eels, Flotsam and
Jetsam, swimming out of the palace window.
"The sea witch has stolen the trident,"
she exclaimed. "I must get it back!"

Ariel covered her ears with shell-muffins and swam to Ursula's lair with the music box. When she arrived, Ursula was boasting about stealing the trident. "Atlantica will be mine!" she shouted. Ariel opened  the music box and watched the strange music send Ursula to sleep. She snatched the trident and swam away.

When Ariel got back to the palace, she used the trident to undo the spell and wake her sisters. "I'm glad I left my trident to watch over you all," said King Triton, when he got home for breakfast. "Princesses can do anything ... even protect a whole kingdom," smiled Ariel. All her sisters agreed, without realising that's what Ariel had done – while they were asleep!

The End

Colour in the pretty seaflowers.

Step into ... Jasmine's World

Here's what you will find:

♥ *Adventurous and generous, Jasmine stands up for what she believes in.*

♥ *Jasmine loves her pet tiger, Rajah. He is a loyal friend.*

♥ *Palace life bored Jasmine. She wanted to have adventures!*

♥ *Abu, Aladdin's monkey, helps his master win Jasmine's heart.*

♥ *Aladdin disguised himself as a prince and took Jasmine on a magic carpet ride.*

♥ *Genie lives in a magic lamp and makes wishes come true!*

Trace the dots around the carpet and colour the picture.

Count the stars, then colour them in.

Magical carpet ride

If I were with Jasmine, we would fly to:

....

Genie Magic

The genie has conjured up some new jewellery for Jasmine using his magic.

a

There are five differences between the pictures. Circle a lamp each time you spot one.

b

Which piece of jewellery do you like the most?

Jasmine's Challenge

*Aladdin has gifts for Jasmine.
But where has he hidden them?*

1

Help Jasmine find her way through the mazes to reach the earrings and tiara.

2

Can you see cheeky Abu?

Start

Colour in this lovely tiara.

Finish

Step into ...
Snow White's World

Here's what you will find:

- Snow White is caring, sweet-natured and friendly to everyone.

- She is very kind to the Seven Dwarfs, who love her dearly.

- The shy forest creatures looked after Snow White when she was lost in the forest.

- The Seven Dwarfs and forest creatures love to hear Snow White sing.

- Snow White's wicked stepmother gave her a poisonous apple.

- A special kiss from The Prince saved Snow White's life.

The birds and Snow White are playing. Finish the picture with some pretty colours.

How many deer can you find?

Gift for a princess

Circle the ring you would choose for Snow White.

Answer on page 61.

Birthday Sparkle

1 It was Snow White's birthday, but the Seven Dwarfs hadn't wished her a happy birthday. When they woke up, they didn't say it. At breakfast, they didn't say it. And when they went to work, they didn't say it.

Goodbye!

Bye, Snow White!

See you tonight!

2 Snow White was sure they had forgotten! "Maybe they'll remember tonight, when I serve them my gooseberry pie," she thought.

3 But the Dwarfs hadn't forgotten at all! While Snow White was baking, they were busy in the mines finding her the perfect birthday gift.

54

Answers on page 61.

4

The Dwarfs found some pretty sapphires. "They're lovely," said Doc. "And beautiful," said Happy. "Just like Snow White," said Bashful, shyly.

5

The Dwarfs got to work making a necklace and earrings out of the beautiful blue stones. Everyone helped except Grumpy.

6

But soon Grumpy stepped up to the work table. "I'll show you how to do it," shouted Grumpy. "We ain't gonna give Snow White her gift until it's perfect!"

Trace the colour of the jewels they found.

blue

7 When the jewellery was ready, Dopey went back to the cottage to trick Snow White into going to the mines. "Something is too high for you to reach?" asked Snow White, and Dopey nodded.

8 When Snow White arrived at the mine, Doc pointed to something sparkly on a high rock. Snow White reached up and carefully lifted it down.

9 To her great surprise it was a sparkling blue necklace and earrings. "How beautiful!" said Snow White. "You remembered my birthday!" "We'd never forget that," said Bashful.

1 Circle the picture of the Dwarf who went to the cottage to bring Snow White back to the mine.

Doc

Dopey

Bashful

Back at the cottage, the Dwarfs made a big birthday celebration! There was music and dancing and Snow White wore her beautiful blue necklace and earrings proudly. She thanked each Dwarf with a kiss – even Grumpy!

The End

2

There are four things wrong in the picture. Can you find:

a Whose hat is wrong?

b Who is playing a broom instead of a guitar?

c Who is using a saw to cut a pie?

d What's wrong with the fire?

Colour in the necklace and make it sparkle.

Quiz Time!

*There's a question for every princess.
Can you answer them all?*

1

Which item would Belle choose for herself:

a

b

c

2

The Fairy Godmother sent Cinderella to the ball in a:

a

b

c

3

Pascal can change his:

a size

b colour

c shape

4

Who cast a sleeping spell on Aurora?

a

b

c

5

Jasmine loves going on adventures!

True

False

6

Who does this shadow belong to?

a

b

7

Tiana runs her own:

a shoe shop

b restaurant

c flower stall

8

How many Dwarfs make friends with Snow White? Trace the number.

6 7

58

Answers on page 61.

Your Pretty Princess Tiara

You can feel like a different princess every time you wear your new tiara!

How to customise your tiara:

1 Cut along the marked line at the bottom of this page.

2 Glue onto a piece of thin cardboard. Leave to dry.

3 Cut along the marked lines around each princess picture.

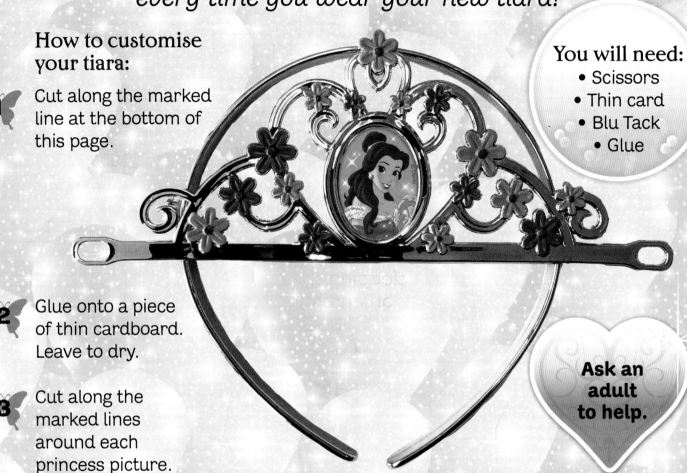

You will need:
- Scissors
- Thin card
- Blu Tack
- Glue

Ask an adult to help.

Cut along here.

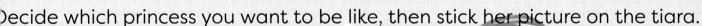

Decide which princess you want to be like, then stick her picture on the tiara.

Confident   Caring   Fun   Kind

Gentle   Creative   Adventurous

Answers

Pages 8-9: Step into … Belle's World
The Wardrobe is hiding behind Belle.

Pages 10-11: In the Palace Garden
1) 4.
2) and 3)

4) b.
5) True.

Pages 12-15: Building Bridges
1) a.
2) c.

Page 16: Fun on the Swing

Page 19: Best Friends
Cinderella's animal friends love her because she is: kind, caring and calm.

Pages 20-21: Step into … Cinderella's World
There are 5 mice.

Pages 22-23: Playful Princess
1) a-4, b-1, c-2, d-3.
2) There are 14 glass slippers.
3) b and e.

Pages 26-27: Step into … Rapunzel's World
Pascal is at the bottom of this page. He is pink!

Page 30: Flower Trail
There are 7 golden flowers.

Page 31: Stand Still, Maximus!
1) a-2, b-4, c-1, d-3.
2) : There are 3 orange and 5 purple butterflies.

Pages 32-33: Step into … Tiana's World
b is Prince Naveen (a is Prince Phillip).

Pages 34-35: It's Snow Time!
a-f, b-d, c-e.

Pages 36-37: Step into … Aurora's World
The smallest rose is a, the biggest rose is c.

Pages 38-41: Merryweather to the Rescue
a-4, b-5, c-2, d-1, e-3.

Pages 42-43: Step into … Ariel's World
Shadow c matches the shell.

Pages 44-45: Happy Birthday!
1) f.
2) 3 jumps.
3) d.
4) Flounder's present is behind the pink sea flowers.

Pages 48-49: Step into … Jasmine's World
There are 6 stars.

Page 50: Genie Magic

Page 51: Jasmine's Challenge
1)

2) Abu is standing on the wall behind Aladdin.

Pages 52-53: Step into … Snow White's World
There are 3 deer.

Pages 54-57: Birthday Sparkle
1) Dopey went to the cottage.
2) a. Grumpy's hat is wrong.
b. Happy is playing a broom rather than a guitar.
c. Dopey is cutting a pie with a saw.
d. The fire is blue instead of orange.

Page 58: Quiz Time!
1) b, 2) a, 3) b, 4) Maleficent, 5) True, 6) Sebastian, 7) b, 8) 7.